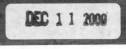

Surf War!

A Folktale from the Marshall Islands

Margaret Read MacDonald
Illustrated by Geraldo Valério

AUGUST HOUSE
Little folk
ATLANTA

Little Sandpiper chased a wave down the beach.
　　Slup … Slup …
She pecked up a tiny fish.
"Here comes another wave!"
Sandpiper ran back up on the beach and waited.
"Now it's going out again …"
Into the water and …
　　Slup … Slup …
Another minnow!

Whale lived deep in this bay.
He thought he ruled the sea.
"You! Little bird! Stay out of my water!
The sea belongs to the WHALES!"

Sandpiper just laughed.
"The sea belongs to the SANDPIPERS too!
And there are lots more sandpipers than whales."

Whale was fuming and spewing.
"More sandpipers?
There are many more WHALES
than sandpipers!"

"Not so! More SANDPIPERS!"

Whale was furious.

"I will call my Whale brothers.
You will see!"

Whale dove deep and called.
"Whales of the EAST!
Whales of the WEST!
Come! Come to my island!"
Whale spouted and dove again.
"Whales of the NORTH!
Whales of the SOUTH!
Come! Come to my island!"

From the east, from the west,
from the north, from the south ...
Whale brothers heard ... Whale brothers came.
Soon that bay was crowded with whales.

Sandpiper was alarmed.
"Just wait! I am going to call my Sandpiper sisters!"

"Sandpipers! Sandpipers!
East and west!
Come quick! Come quick to my island!

"Sandpipers! Sandpipers!
North and south!
Come quick! Come quick to my island!"

From the east, from the west,
from the north, from the south ...
Sandpipers came flying!
Soon birds covered the beach!

Were there more birds?
Or more whales?
More whales?
Or more birds?
It was impossible to say.

"We need our COUSINS!"

So the whales all dove deep and called,
    "Cousins to the EAST!
    Cousins to the WEST!
    Come! Come to our island!

    "Cousins to the NORTH!
    Cousins to the SOUTH!
    Come! Come to our island!"

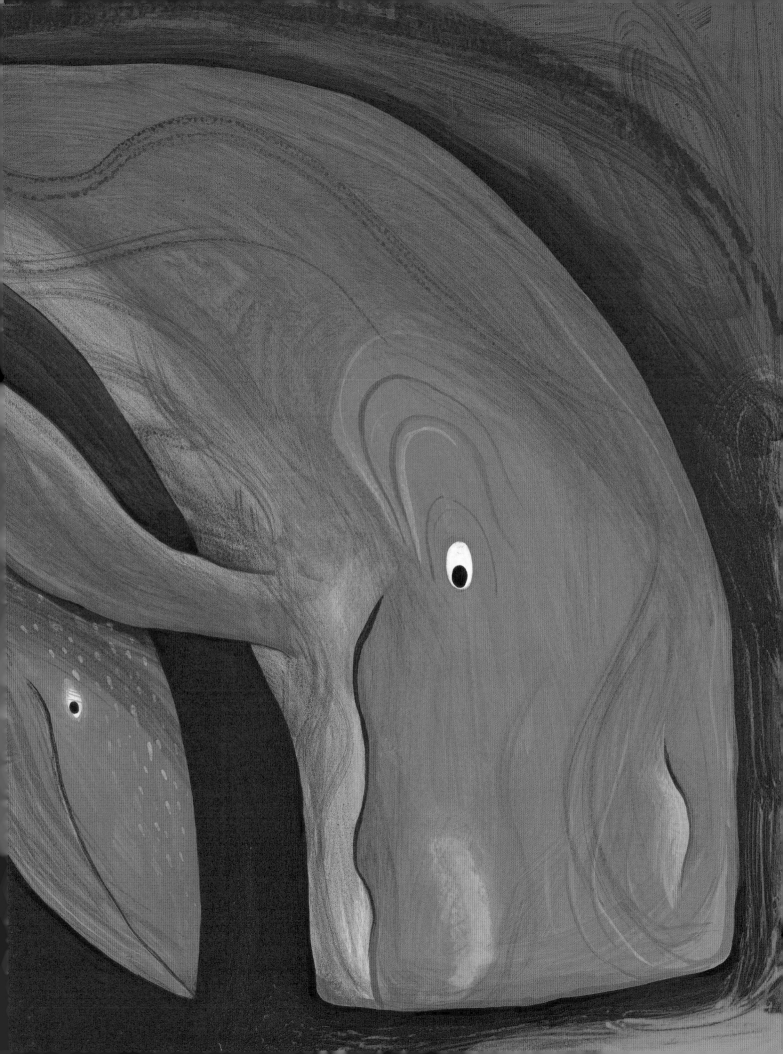

From the east, from the west,
from the north, from the south …
Dolphins, orcas, porpoises …
Whale cousins heard, and whale cousins came.

The island was now surrounded
by whales and whale cousins.

"Quick! Call OUR cousins too!
Sandpiper cousins!
East and west!
Come quick! Come quick to our island!

"Sandpiper cousins!
North and south!
Come quick! Come quick to our island!"

From the east, from the west,
from the north, from the south …
Sandpiper cousins came.
Flamingos, pelicans, egrets, terns …
Every inch of that island
was covered by birds!

Were there more birds or more whales?
More whales or more birds?

It was impossible to say.

Then Whale had an idea.
"If the whales eat up all the land …
those birds will have no place to perch!
Then there will be more whales than sandpipers!
Let's DO IT!"

Scrunch! Scrunch!

The whales began to munch on the beach.
Scrunch! Scrunch!
The beach was being torn away by their huge jaws.

Then Sandpiper had an idea.
"If we birds drink up the sea …
there will be no water for the whales!
Then there will be more sandpipers
than whales!

Let's DO IT!"

Each bird dipped its beak in the sea.
Each bird began to drink.

Slurp ...

Sluurp ...
Sluuurp ...

The whales were munching.
The birds were slurping.
But it is easier to slurp than to munch.
The birds were winning.

Fish were gasping for breath.
Tiny crabs, starfish, sea creatures
were dying in the hot sun.

"Stop!" cried Sandpiper. "STOP!"

"Those tiny crabs! Those little minnows!
That is our food!" said Sandpiper.
"If THEY die ... WE die too!
Spit back the water!"

Ptoooie ...
ptoooie ...
ptoooie ...

The sea creatures all revived and swam away.

"Stop!" bellowed Whale. "STOP!
The beach is part of our ocean.
We are destroying our home!
Spit back the land!"

Glurk …
Glurk …
Glurk …

The whales spat back the beach.

"This war was not a good thing," said Whale.
"We need to take care of our sea."

"Agreed," said Sandpiper. "There is plenty of ocean to share."

So the whales and their cousins swam away …
to the east, to the west, to the north, to the south.
The sandpipers and their cousins flew away …
to the east, to the west, to the north, to the south.

And no one ever knew …
Were there more whales or more birds?
More birds or more whales?
Such a silly thing to start a war.

So Whale and Sandpiper settled
down to share and care for their
beautiful bay ... together.

For Matilda and Cordelia; may they share and care for their
beautiful Guemes Island bay together—**MRM**

For Marshequa and Chantrelle—**GV**

About the Story

Variants of this story appear in *Legends of the South Seas, Book I* by Eve Grey
(Honolulu: Island Import Company, 1954) and in *The Magic Calabash* by Jean Cothran
(New York: David McKay, 1954). An earlier version appears in *Peace Tales: World Folktales
to Talk About* by Margaret Read MacDonald (Little Rock: August House, 2006). The tale is
a variant of Motif B250 *Animal warfare*.

Eve Grey writes that in the Marshall Islands the story was used as a bedtime tale.
The grandparent would just keep calling in more birds and more sea creatures until the
child fell asleep!

Text copyright © 2009 by Margaret Read MacDonald
Illustrations copyright © 2009 by Geraldo Valério

Published 2009 by August House LittleFolk
3500 Piedmont Road NE, Suite 310, Atlanta, Georgia 30305,
404-442-4420
http://www.augusthouse.com

Manufactured in Korea

10 9 8 7 6 5 4 3 2 1

LIBRARY OF CONGRESS CATALOGING-IN-PUBLICATION DATA

MacDonald, Margaret Read, 1940-
Surf war! : a folktale from the Marshall Islands / Margaret Read MacDonald ;
illustrated by Geraldo Valério.
p. cm.
Summary: A bragging contest between Whale and Sandpiper turns into a
battle over the beach and sea, until both parties realize that the beach and
the sea, as well as sea creatures and shorebirds, are interdependent.
ISBN 978-0-87483-889-3 (hardcover : alk. paper)
[1. Folklore--Marshall Islands. 2. Ecology--Folklore.] I. Valério,
Geraldo, 1970- ill. II. Title.

PZ8.1.M15924Su 2009
398.209683--dc22
[E]
2008042589

The paper used in this publication meets the minimum requirements of the American National Standard for
Information Sciences—Permanence of Paper for Printed Library Materials,
ANSI Z39.48-1984